I Feel...

DIFFERENT

Words and pictures by

DJ Corchin

sourcebooks
eXplore

Sometimes I feel **different.**

Like I'm slightly **too tall**.

Or unusually **big,**

and I **don't fit** at all.

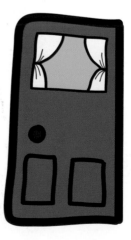

Sometimes it may seem that I made the **wrong** call,

Sometimes I feel **odd**

'cause I have a **weird** tooth.

Or when everyone **lies**,
and I tell the **truth**.

Sometimes I'm **unique**
'cause I have a pet goose.

All my friends are **acute**,

while I am **obtuse**.

I'm not that outgoing.
I'm unusually **shy**.

It might be because
of my **gargantuan** eye.

Sometimes I feel **lonely**,
and I happen to cry.

But I'm amazingly **smart**,

and now I can **fly**.

Sometimes I'm **outnumbered**
'cause of my particular view

and standing alone

vs.

seems the wrong thing to do.

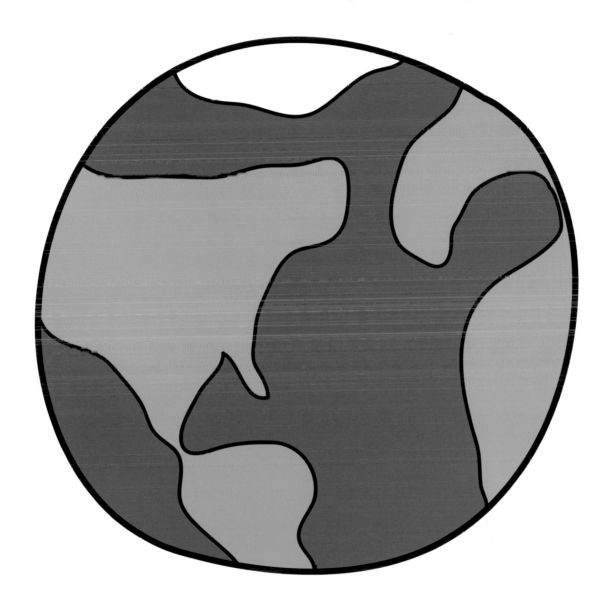

When everyone **clucks**,

and I want to **moo**,

sometimes it feels **tough**,
like I don't have a clue.

But the voice that's inside me is **proud** of those traits.

It tells me I'm **special**.
It tells me I'm **great**.

I like that I'm **different**
so people can see,

that the reasons I'm different
are the reasons **I'm me**.

I Feel...
DIFFERENT

We all are different in so many ways! What makes us different and unique is what makes us, well, us. It's important to get to know these differences, embrace them, and even love them. Our similarities may bring us together, but it's our differences that make us stronger. Let's celebrate our differences with each other!

There are lots of ways to be or feel different. Different is good!

What makes you feel different? Let's identify it!

1. Is it something you can see, say, or hear?

2. Is it something about your body?

3. Does it have to do with your friends?

4. Does it have to do with your family?

5. Does it make you feel happy or sad?

6. Do you know anyone else who may feel different in the same way?

It is ALWAYS OK to ask someone for help when you are feeling bad.

The I Feel... Children's Series is a resource created to assist in discussions about emotional awareness.

Please seek the help of a trained mental healthcare professional and start a discussion today.

Make your own Book of Different:

1. Make a list of five to ten friends, family, or classmates.

2. Write each of their names on the top of a separate piece of paper.

3. Draw a single, large triangle in the middle of the page.

4. Ask each person what is one thing that makes them different.

5. Draw them as an I Feel... triangle face on the paper with their name on it.

6. Be sure to show what makes them different.

7. Use tape or a stapler to combine the pages into a book.

8. Whenever you're feeling uncomfortable about what makes you different, read your new Book of Different about your friends and family and remember, we all have unique things about us that make us who we are.

Listen to a symphony orchestra:

1. How many different types of instruments do you hear?

2. Can you name any of the instruments you hear?

3. Do you hear any sounds that you don't recognize?

4. How would it sound if every instrument were the same?

5. Partner with an adult to discover as many instruments as you can find. What do they look like? How do they sound?

A history of different:

1. Partner with an adult and make a list of five people in history you'd like to know more about.

2. Visit your local library and find books on each of these people.

3. Discover what might be different about these people and if it helped them accomplish their goals.

4. You could draw them as I Feel... triangle faces and add them to your Book of Different!

To Mike

Published by Sourcebooks eXplore, an imprint of Sourcebooks Kids
P.O. Box 4410, Naperville, Illinois 60567–4410
(630) 961-3900
sourcebookskids.com

Originally published in 2011 in the United States of America by The phazelFOZ Company, LLC.

Library of Congress Cataloging-in-Publication Data is on file with the publisher.

Source of Production: 1010 Printing Asia Limited, North Point, Hong Kong, China
Date of Production: July 2020
Run Number: 5019075

Printed and bound in China.
OGP 10 9 8 7 6 5 4 3 2 1